Tara Fass, LMFT

Judith A. Proffer

When We Stayed Home

Illustrated by Yoko Matsuoka

When We Stayed Home

Copyright 2020 Tara Fass LMFT and Judith A. Proffer

ISBN: 978-1-7353844-1-2

First published in 2020 by Huqua Press
An operating unit of Morling Manor Corporation
Los Angeles, California

Graphic Design: designSimple

huquapress.com

For Lucas, and
for all the children
who stayed home

Oh, hi.

It's me behind the polka dots.

This is my story of when we stayed home.

When a scary virus traveled all over the world, we stayed home to help the helpers.

And when we stayed home, we became helpers too.

That's me, a super-helper!

Super-helpers do a lot.

When we stayed home we washed our hands.

All. The. Time.

I wore a mask when I was outdoors and near people who don't live in my house.

Sometimes the mask was scratchy and stuffy and not like a super hero mask at all.

It was a super-helper mask, so I only grumbled a little.

When we stayed home I built
a million forts, my special space
where no masks were required
and no virus was allowed.

When we stayed home I fished in the garden under a bluer-than-usual sky.

When we stayed home I did crazy things with my hair.

And I made silly faces too.

When we stayed home
I decorated cookies to drop
off on my neighbors' front
porch.

They were staying home too.

It's what super-helpers do.

When we stayed home I had so many screen visits with family and friends.

They always had smiles to see me.

Sometimes their eyeballs leaked tears.

We had zippy dance parties too.

Even my auntie danced with me.

She was tiny on the phone but I could tell she was trying hard to keep up with my moves.

When we stayed home I peeked out the window every day to see neighbors walk their dogs.

I always gave them my biggest super-helper smile and a friendly wave hello.

I think it made them happy behind their masks.

When we stayed home
I did schoolwork and learned
so many new things.

Like which snacks go best
with math.

When we stayed home
I painted what was living in
my dreams.

When we stayed home I was
sometimes artsy with my food.

I also did
puzzles to keep
my super-helper
brain thinking
and growing.

When we stayed home I drew a rocket ship on the sidewalk.

We couldn't go very far from home but that didn't stop me from soaring to the moon.

When we stayed home we all read lots and lots of books.

Sometimes they took me to faraway places too.

When we stayed home I thought about everyone and everything I missed.

Even super-helpers are sad every now and then.

I missed being with my friends
in real life.

I missed my teacher and classroom and going to school.

I missed going to the park and playing on the playground.

Most of all, I missed seeing my family and friends who were staying home in other houses.

Oh, how I missed their hugs and kisses.

When we stayed home I tried not to think too much about what I missed, because my trusty imagination kicked in when I needed it most.

When the real super heroes around the world were helping us all, I wore a mask, I washed my hands, and I stayed home.

You probably did too.

One more thing I have to say:

When we stayed home I didn't have everything I wanted.

But I had everything I needed.

Core Knowledge Language Arts®

Unit 3
Workbook

Skills Strand
GRADE 1

Amplify learning.

Core Knowledge®

ISBN 978-1-61700-202-1

Printed in the USA
08 LSCOW 2021

Unit 3
Workbook

This Workbook contains worksheets that accompany many of the lessons from the *Teacher Guide* for Unit 3. Each worksheet is identified by the lesson number in which it is used. The worksheets in this book do not include written instructions for students because the instructions would have words that are not decodable. Teachers will explain these worksheets to the students orally, using the instructions in the Teacher Guide. The Workbook is a student component, which means each student should have a Workbook.

Spelling Words

1. s<u>a</u>m<u>e</u>

2. gr<u>ee</u>n

3. st<u>o</u>n<u>e</u>

4. l<u>i</u>n<u>e</u>

5. m<u>a</u>k<u>e</u>

6. h<u>i</u>d<u>e</u>

7. s<u>ee</u>d

8. Tricky Word: they

Dear Family Member,

Today we started Unit 3 of Core Knowledge Language Arts. Starting with this unit, your child will receive a new list of spelling words each Monday. The purpose of having weekly spelling words is to help students become strong spellers and allow them to practice at home the skills learned during Core Knowledge Language Arts. Your child will receive the spelling words at the beginning of the week and will be tested on the words at the end of the week.

There are eight words each week. The words cover only the spellings that have been reviewed and taught in class, meaning that your child will only work with and be tested on familiar spellings. The last spelling word is shaded in gray to indicate it is a Tricky Word. Tricky Words do not follow the expected spelling rules, so they cannot be reliably sounded out and spelled, which means their spellings must be memorized. Tricky Words are also taught and reviewed in class.

I encourage you to work with your child each night to review the spelling words for 5–10 minutes. The activities can be fun but should involve having your child write the word, not just spelling it aloud.

Here are a few activity ideas:

- Say a sentence with the spelling word, but leave the spelling word out. Your child should guess which of the week's spelling words should complete the sentence and then write the word down.

- Create spelling word flash cards. After reading the word on a flash card, your child can turn over the card and write the word from memory on another piece of paper.

- Have a spelling bee at home, asking your child to both spell the words to you orally and write them.

- Ask your child to write each word in a short sentence, or write a story with the words.

- If possible, act out or draw a picture of the words; have your child guess the word and then write it down.

- Please have your child practice spelling the words in a different order each night; do not simply call them out in the order listed.

- Starting later this week, your child will also bring home a story that we have read in class. The story for this week is called "King Log and King Crane." Please have your child read the story to you and then talk about it together.

If you have any questions, please do not hesitate to contact me.

OO

Directions: Have students trace and copy the digraph and words. Students should say the sounds while writing the letters.

oo oo . . . . .

oo . . . . .

soon soon

soon

loot loot

loot

room room

room

In the box are nine words. Print them on the lines where they fit best.

moon	tooth	broom
roots	loop	tools
food	spoon	boots

moon

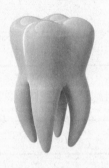

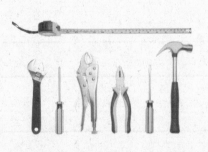

King Log and King Crane

1. What did the frogs ask the gods to send them?

   ○ lots of f**oo**d

   ○ a log

   ○ a king

   Page _____

2. Did the frogs like King Log? <u>Why</u> or <u>why</u> not?

   _____
   _____
   _____
   _____
   _____
   _____
   _____

   Page _____

Directions: Students should reread the story and answer the questions, noting the page number where they found the answer.

3. Did the frogs like King Crane? <u>Why</u> or <u>why</u> not?

_____

_____

_____

_____

_____

_____

_____

Page _____

4. <u>Who</u> was mad in the end?

○ King Log

○ the gods

○ the frogs

Page _____

Directions: Have students fill in the story map to describe the characters, setting, and plot of the story.

The Name of the Tale:

Who?

Where?

What?

Once, there were...

Next in the tale...

At the end of the tale...

Name _____

Dear Family Member,
This is a story your child has probably read once, possibly several times at school. Encourage your child to read the story to you and then talk about it together. Note that the tricky parts in Tricky Words are underlined in gray. Repeated reading is an important way to improve reading. It can be fun for your child to repeatedly read this story to a friend, relative, or even a pet.

King Log and King Crane

Once the frogs said, "We wish we had a king! We need a king! We must have a king!"

The frogs spoke to the gods. They said, "We ask you, the gods, to send us a king!"

"The frogs are fools," said the gods. "As a joke, let us send them a big log to be their king."

The gods got a big log and let it drop. The log fell in the pond and made a big splash.

The frogs were scared of the log. They said, "King Log is strong! We must hide from him in the grass!"

As time went by, the frogs came to see that King Log was

tame. He did not bite. He did not run. He just sat there.

"King Log is not a strong king!" said one frog.

"I wish we had a strong king!"

"I do, too!"

"We must have a strong king!"

The frogs spoke to the gods. They said, "We ask you, the gods, to send us a strong king, and send him soon!"

This time the gods sent a crane to be king of Frog Land.

King Crane was not like King Log. He did not just sit there. He ran fast on his long legs, and he ate lots of the frogs.

The frogs were sad.

"King Crane is a bad king," they said. "We miss King Log! He was a fine king. We made a bad trade!"

The frogs spoke to the gods. They said, "We ask you, the gods, to send us back King Log!"

The gods were mad. "Fools!" they said. "You said you must have a strong king. We sent you one. He is yours to keep!"

The Two Dogs

1. Which dog gets food from the men?
   - ○ the tame dog
   - ○ the dog who runs free

Page _____

2. Why is one dog plump?

_____

_____

_____

_____

_____

_____

Page _____

3. What makes the thin dog run off?

4.

Spelling Test

1. _____

2. _____

3. _____

4. _____

5. _____

6. _____

7. _____

8. _____

Name _____

Directions: Have students trace and copy the digraph and words. Students should say the sounds while writing the letters.

oo oo . . . .

oo . . . .

look

foot

good

In the box are six words. Print them on the lines where they fit best.

br**oo**k	b**oo**k	h**oo**d
f**oo**t	h**oo**k	c**oo**k

_____

_____

_____

_____

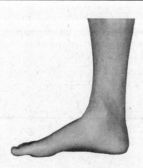

_____

_____

Dear Family Member,
This is a story your child has probably read once, possibly several times at
school. Encourage your child to read the story to you and then talk about it
together. Note that the tricky parts in Tricky Words are underlined in gray.
Repeated reading is an important way to improve reading. It can be fun for
your child to repeatedly read this story to a friend, relative, or even a pet.

The Two Dogs

Once two dogs met. One of
them was a tame dog who made
his home with men. One was a
dog who ran free.

The dog who ran free stared
at the tame dog and said, "Why is it
that you are so plump and I am so
thin?"

"Well," said the tame dog, "I am
plump because the men feed me.
I do not have to run all the time to
get my food. My job is to keep the
home safe when the men are in
their beds. When they wake
up, they feed me scraps of food
from their plates."

"Your life must be a fine life,"
said the thin dog. "I wish my life
were like yours."

The plump dog said, "If you will help me keep the home safe, I bet the men will feed you, too."

"I will do it!" said the thin dog.

But just as the thin dog said this, the moon shone on the neck of the plump dog.

The thin dog said, "What is that on your neck?"

"I am on a rope when the sun is up," said the plump dog.

"Rope?" said the thin dog. "Do they keep you on a rope?"

"Yes," said the plump dog. "When the moon is up, the men let me run free, but when the sun shines, they keep me on a rope. I can not run and be free when the sun shines, but it is not so bad."

"No, no!" said the thin dog, as he ran off. "I will not have a rope on my neck. You can be plump. I will be free!"

Dear Family Member,

This week during our language arts time, we will continue to explore the writing process with students. We are teaching students to plan, draft and edit written compositions before creating a final product. Ask your child to explain the process to you.

We will also continue to read stories from the reader *Fables*. Your child can explain the different morals from the stories we read in class.

Included below are the spelling words for this week. Remember to encourage your child to practice these words each night in order to be prepared for the test at the end of the week.

Spelling Words

1. frog

2. moth

3. quote

4. wood

5. took

6. spoon

7. tooth

8. Tricky Word: why

Name _____

Directions: Have students fill in the story map to describe the characters, setting, and plot of the story.

The Name of the Tale:

<u>Who?</u>

<u>Where?</u>

What?

<u>Once</u>, there w<u>ere</u>...

Next in the tale...

At the end of the tale...

The Name of the Tale: _____

In the tale, "The Two Dogs," _____

_____

_____

_____

Once _____

_____

_____

_____

Next, _____

_____

_____

_____

Directions: Have students use the template for their book reports.

In the end _____

_____

_____

_____

This tale tells us _____

_____

_____

_____

I liked/did not like this tale because _____

_____

_____

_____

The Hares and Frogs

Directions: Have students reread the story and answer the questions. Tell them to record the page on which they found their answer.

1. <u>Where</u> did the hares h<u>a</u>ve a chat?
   - ○ in the grass
   - ○ in a tree
   - ○ in a hut

   Page_____

2. <u>Why</u> w<u>ere</u> t<u>wo</u> of the hares sad?
   - ○ They were f**oo**ls.
   - ○ They were tame.
   - ○ They were not brave.

   Page_____

3. What are some things that scare the hares?

_____

_____

_____

_____

Page _____

4. Who was scared of the hares in the end?

_____

_____

_____

_____

Page _____

oo

① /oo/ as in soon   ② /oo/ as in look

~~boo~~	~~book~~	bloom	food
took	cool	good	cook

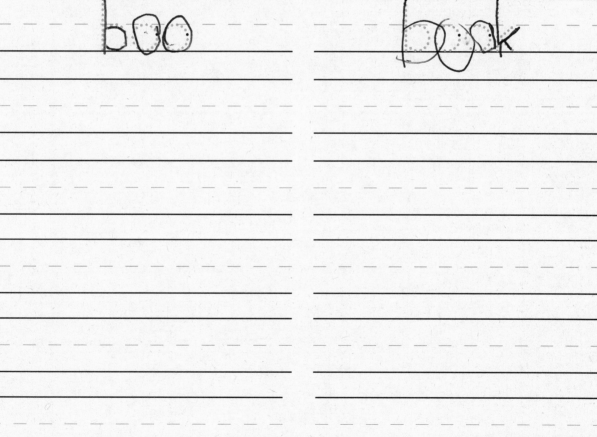

/oo/ as in boo   /oo/ as in book

boo

book

Directions: Read the words aloud as a class. Have students write the words with the /oo/ sound under the 'boo' header and the words with the /oo/ sound under the 'book' header.

Dear Family Member:

Your child has been taught to read words with the vowel sounds /oo/ as in *soon* and /oo/ as in *look*. Reading words like these is tricky because the two vowel sounds are spelled with the exact same spelling, 'oo' but pronounced differently. Ask your child to cut out the word cards. Show the cards to your child and have your child read them. You may also ask your child to copy the words onto a sheet of paper. Your child can sort the word cards into two piles: one pile for words with /oo/ as in *soon* and one pile for words with /oo/ as in *look*. Please keep and use the cards for future practice.

pool	moon	cook
look	foot	hood
food	boot	book
spoon	took	root

The Two Mules

| spots | strong | ten | packs |
| five | mules | lift | **f**oo**l** |

A man went on a trip with two _____.

The black mule was _____, but the

mule with _____ was not as strong.

The mule with spots had to ask the black mule to help him with

his _____. "I have my five packs and

you have your _____," said the black mule. The

mule with spots went on, but at last he fell and could not get up.

The man set all _____ packs on the black mule.

The black mule said, "What a _____ I was!

I did not help the mule with spots when I should have! If I had,

I would not have to _____ all of his

packs as well as mine."

Name _____

ou

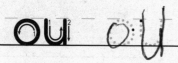

ou ou

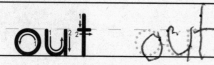

out out

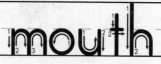

mouth

shout

© 2013 Core Knowledge Foundation

Directions: Have students trace and copy the digraphs and words. Students should say the sounds while writing the letters.

Print the words on the lines where they fit best.

1. cl**ou**d

_____

- - - - - - - - - - - -

_____

2. sn**ou**t

_____

- - - - - - - - - - - -

_____

3. m**ou**th

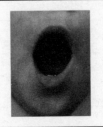

_____

- - - - - - - - - - - -

_____

4. c**ou**ch

_____

- - - - - - - - - - - -

_____

5. r**ou**nd

_____

- - - - - - - - - - - -

_____

Spelling Test

1. _____

2. _____

3. _____

4. _____

5. _____

6. _____

7. _____

8. _____

 _____

_____

1. <u>run</u> up the hill

2. mop the r**oo**m

3. c**oo**k g**oo**d f**oo**d

4. l**oo**k it up

5. shake his hand

6. pet the dog

run

Directions: Have students cut out the events from the story "The Dog and the Mule." Tell them to look back at their Reader to find the correct order of events. They will then tape or glue the events in the right order on the next page.

The Dog and the Mule

The mule gave the man a big lick and set his feet on the man's lap.

The man let the dog lick him and his sp**oo**n. The man would rub the dog and kiss him.

The man was scared. He made the mule run back **ou**t to his pen.

The mule felt left **ou**t. The mule said, "I sh**ou**ld act like a dog."

A man had a dog and a mule.

Name _____

The Dog and the Mule

Name _____

Dear Family Member,
This is a story your child has probably read once, possibly several times at school. Encourage your child to read the story to you and then talk about it together. Note that the tricky parts in Tricky Words are underlined in gray. Repeated reading is an important way to improve reading. It can be fun for your child to repeatedly read this story to a friend, relative, or even a pet.

The Hares and the Frogs

Three hares st**oo**d in the grass.

"I am sad," one of them said. "I wish we were brave."

"So do I," said the next one. "But we are not brave. A splash in the br**oo**k scares us. The wind in the grass scares us. We are scared all the time."

"Yes," said the last one. "It is sad to be a hare."

Just then there was a splash in the brook. The splash scared the hares. They ran off to hide. As they ran, they scared a bunch of frogs.

"Look," said one of the hares. "The frogs are scared of us!"

"Yes, they are!" said the next hare. "They are scared of us! Well, I'm glad I am not a frog!"

"Yes!" said the last hare. "In the end, it is good to be a hare!"

Spelling Words

1. brook

2. stood

3. booth

4. room

5. south

6. proud

7. shout

8. Tricky Word: down

Yes? No?

1. Can a **rou**nd sp**oo**n fit in y**our** m**ou**th?

_____
_____
_____

2. Is there a **cou**ch in the r**oo**m?

_____
_____
_____

3. Are there big cats at the z**oo**?

_____
_____
_____

4. Can you wave y**our** hand to sh**oo** a bug?

_____
_____
_____

5. Can you **cou**nt the b**oo**ks?

_____
_____
_____

6. Is the gr**ou**nd d**ow**n?

_____
_____
_____

7. Is a cake sweet?

_____
_____
_____

8. Can a mule **coo**k f**oo**d?

_____
_____

_____

here they fit best.

shout	free	
need	spoon	
food	feet	fools

_____ a king!"

ogs were _____.

his _____ from men.

to be _____.

slash in the _____.

6. _____ were scared all the time.

7. mule did not help the mule with spots with his

_____.

let the dog lick his _____.

his _____ on the man's lap.

_____ and he was scared.

The Bag of Coins

1. What did the man <u>who</u> f**ou**nd the c**oi**ns tell the next man?

_____

Page_____

2. <u>Why</u> was the mob mad?

_____

3. When the mob came, the man with the coins said, "If they see us with the coins, . . .

○ they will be glad."

○ they will be scared."

○ we will be in a bad spot."

Page_____

Directions: In the box, have students illustrate a part of the story and write a caption below.

Dear Family Member:

Your child has been taught to read words with the vowel spellings 'oo' as in *spoon*, 'oo' as in *book*, 'ou' as in *cloud*, and 'oi' as in *boil*. Ask your child to cut out the word cards. Show the cards to your child and have your child read them. Then have your child read the word cards from previous take-home worksheets. You may ask your child to copy the words onto a sheet of paper. In addition, you can read the words aloud and have your child write the words down, one sound at a time, paying attention to the digraphs. Please keep the cards for future practice.

smooth	moon	round
cook	boil	foil
look	spoon	loud
sound	book	oil

Directions: For each word, have students circle and count the spellings, then write the number of sounds in the box, and copy the word on the lines.

1. c**oi**ns

2. m**oi**st

3. br**oo**m

4. t**oo**th

5. sc**oo**p

6. c**ou**ch

7. sh**oo**k

8. j**oi**nt

9. cr**ou**ch

10. f**ou**l

11. h**oo**d

12. st**oo**p

13. tr**oo**p

14. p**oi**nt

15. dr**oo**p

16. m**ou**nt

Spelling Test

1. _____

2. _____

3. _____

4. _____

5. _____

6. _____

7. _____

8. _____

_____

Directions: Have students trace and copy the digraphs and words. Students should say the sounds while writing the letters.

aw   aw

aw

draw   draw

draw

saw   saw

saw

paw   paw

paw

Print the words on the lines where they fit best.

1. cl**aw**

_____
- - - - - - - - - - -
_____

2. p**aw**

_____
- - - - - - - - - - -
_____

3. s**aw**

_____
- - - - - - - - - - -
_____

4. l**aw**n

_____
- - - - - - - - - - -
_____

5. cr**aw**l

_____
- - - - - - - - - - -
_____

The Dog and the Ox

Directions: Have students reread the story and answer the questions.

1. <u>Where</u> did the dog take his nap?

   ○ in a loft

   ○ in a den

   ○ in a f**oo**d box

   Page____

2. What did the dog d<u>o</u> when the ox came back?

   ○ He got off the str**aw**.

   ○ He did not get off the str**aw**.

   ○ He went to the loft.

   Page_____

3. <u>Why</u> did the dog get off of the str**aw** in the end?

    ○ The dog was mad.

    ○ The ox said he c<u>ou</u>ld sleep in the loft.

    ○ The man said the dog must get up.

Page_____

Name _____

Dear Family Member:

For Unit 3 of our Core Knowledge Language Arts program, your child has been taught to read the Tricky Words *should*, *could*, *would*, *because*, and *down*. Tricky Words are hard to read because they contain parts that are not pronounced the way one would expect. For this reason, students must memorize the word.

Have your child read the Tricky Words in the box and then the sentences below. Note that the tricky parts are underlined in gray. Have your child write the matching Tricky Word for each sentence and write it on the line. Please note that there could be different answers for the sentences. Ask your child to read the completed sentence out loud, and ask if it makes sense. You may ask your child if there is another word that could fit in the sentence as well.

should	could	would	because	down

1. You _____ wash your hands.

2. _____ you hand me that?

3. I was glad _____ I ate cake for

    lunch.

4. I _____ jump up and sing.

5. The stars are up, not _____ .

Unit 3 **67**
© 2013 Core Knowledge Foundation

1.  cook | 3 |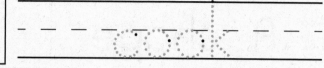

2. cloud | |

3. lawn | |

4. point | |

5. sleep | |

6. spoon | |

7. brook | |

8. moist | |

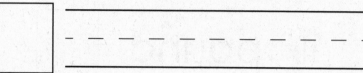

9. shape

10. hawk

11. pound

12. saw

13. pool

14. join

15. shout

16. wood

Dear Family Member,
This is a story your child has probably read once, possibly several times at school. Encourage your child to read the story to you and then talk about it together. Note that the tricky parts in Tricky Words are underlined in gray. Repeated reading is an important way to improve reading. It can be fun for your child to repeatedly read this story to a friend, relative, or even a pet.

The Dog and the Ox

Once a dog took a nap on a pile of straw in a box. But the straw in the box was not a bed.

When the ox came home, he saw the straw in his food box. But he could not get to the straw because the dog was on top of it.

"Dog," said the ox, "could you sleep up in the loft? I would like to munch on the straw in my food box."

The dog woke up, but he would not get off the straw. He was mad that the ox woke him up.

At last, a man came in and saw the dog on the straw.

"Bad dog!" said the man. "You did not need that straw, but you would not let the ox have it! Shame on you! Get up!"

Directions: Have students copy the word onto the left side of the paper, fold it in half, and then write the word from memory on the right side of the paper.

1. _____

2. _____

3. _____

4. _____

5. _____

6. _____

7. _____

8. _____

9. _____

10. _____

1. _____

2. _____

3. _____

4. _____

5. _____

6. _____

7. _____

8. _____

9. _____

10. _____

The Fox and the Grapes

1. What did the fox see?

   ○ a fat hen

   ○ a f**aw**n

   ○ a bunch of ripe grapes

   Page_____

2. To get the grapes, the fox . . .

   _____

   _____

   _____

   _____

   _____

   _____

   _____

   _____

   Page_____

Directions: Have students reread the story and answer the questions.

3. Can the fox tell that the grapes are **sou**r? <u>Why</u> or <u>why</u> not?

_____

- -

_____

- -

_____

- -

_____

- -

_____

Page_____

Directions: In the box, have students illustrate a part of the story and write a caption below.

Directions: Have students circle the word their teacher says.

1.   punt   point   put   pout

2.   wood   want   wool   wet

3.   foil   food   foot   fed

4.   clam   clod   coil   cloud

5.   foil   fall   for   fell

6.   mouth   moist   mount   moth

7.   shout   shine   soil   shoot

8.   look   lake   loot   late

9.	clap	cot	couch	coil
10.	joust	jar	Jill	join
11.	south	smooth	sand	smooch
12.	male	mouth	mill	mope
13.	shell	shout	share	shook
14.	boot	bout	bite	boon
15.	stand	stood	shout	store

The Fox and the Crane

1. The fox asks the crane to have:

   ○ lunch with him

   ○ fun with him

   ○ a snack with him

2. The fox was up to a trick. He gave the crane s<u>o</u>m<u>e</u> food:

   ○ in a flat stone dish

   ○ on big plate

   ○ in a bag

3. The crane c<u>ou</u>ld not get the f**oo**d be<u>cau</u>se:

   ○ he did not like it

   ○ of the shape of his bill

   ○ the dish was hot

4. The crane gave the milk to the fox:

○ on a big plate

○ in a flat stone dish

○ in a glass with a long, thin neck

5. The fox could not get the milk because:

○ the milk was bad

○ of the shape of his nose

○ of the shape of his bill

6. The tale tells us what?

○ If you trick a pal, he could trick you.

○ Milk is best from a tall glass.

○ A long bill is best.

pool   sh<u>oo</u>k   tool   cook

hook   zoom   smooth   took

/<u>oo</u>/ as in b**oo**   /oo/ as in b**oo**k

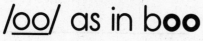

Directions: Have students write the words with the /oo/ sound under the 'boo' header and the words with the /oo/ sound under the 'book' header.

cute	hoop
cube	use
room	soon
mute	loop

/ue/ as in c<u>u</u>t<u>e</u>

cute

/oo/ as in c<u>oo</u>l

hoop

~~boil~~	~~loud~~
join	round
sound	hoist
moist	foul

/oi/ as in oil   /ou/ as in shout

boil   loud

Directions: Have students write the words with the /oi/ sound under the 'oil' header and the words with the /ou/ sound under the 'shout' header.

Directions: For each word, have students circle and count the spellings, then write the number of sounds in the box, and copy the word on the lines.

1. claws

| 4 |

claws

2. hoist

3. hoop

4. loud

5. shook

6. draw

7. oil

8. shout

9. g**oo**d

10. m**ou**th

11. h**oo**d

12. y**aw**n

13. p**o**int

14. pr**ou**d

15. p**aw**

16. l**oo**k

Name _____

Print the words.

cool   cool

moon   moon

root   root

hoop   hoop

scoop   scoop

Print the words.

look   look

foot   foot

good   good

hood   hood

nook   nook

Print the words.

loud   loud

shout   shout

couch   couch

mouth   mouth

round   round

Print the words.

joint   joint

soil   soil

coin   coin

foil   foil

point   point

Print the words.

law   law

straw   straw

paw   paw

yawn   yawn

shawl   shawl

Directions: Have students copy the word onto the left side of the paper, fold it in half, and then write the word from memory on the right side of the paper.

1. _____

2. _____

3. _____

4. _____

5. _____

6. _____

7. _____

8. _____

9. _____

10. _____

1. _____

2. _____

3. _____

4. _____

5. _____

6. _____

7. _____

8. _____

9. _____

10. _____

Print the words.

because   because

would   would

could   could

should   should

down   down

Print the words.

because

would

could

should

down

1. Is the m**oo**n made **ou**t of cake?

no

2. Can a duck squ**aw**k?

3. Can a h**aw**k sw**oo**p down?

4. Is str**aw** a f**oo**d?

5. Are y<u>ou</u>r pants made **ou**t of tin f**oi**l?

6. Is a dime a c**oi**n?

7. Is there f**oo**d on the gr**ou**nd?

8. D<u>o</u> you like to l**oo**k at b**oo**ks?

Directions: Have students answer the questions by writing 'yes' or 'no' on the lines.

9. Is two plus two six?

         _____

10. Can a hawk coil up like a snake?

         _____

11. Do we use oil to cook?

         _____

12. Can you crawl as fast as you can run?

         _____

13. Can you draw the sun?

         _____

14. Can you jump on one foot?

         _____

15. Can a broom sing a song?

         _____

16. Do you have a green couch in your home?

         _____

In the box are nine words. Print them on the lines where they fit best.

y**aw**n	sp**oo**n	sp**ou**t
f**oo**t	c**oi**n	cr**aw**l
b**oo**k	c**ou**ch	br**oo**m

_____

_____

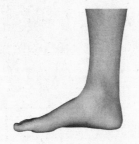

_____

_____

_____

_____

In the box are nine words. Print them on the lines where they fit best.

t**oo**ls	c**oi**l	h**oo**k
m**ou**th	h**aw**k	p**aw**
s**oi**l	t**oo**th	b**oo**ts

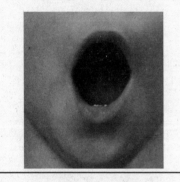

_____

_____

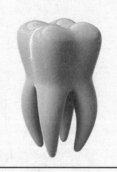

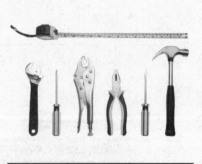

_____

_____

_____

_____

Print the words on the lines where they fit best.

1. f**oo**d

_____   _____

- - - - - - - - - - - - -   - - - - - - - - - - - - -

_____   _____

2. cl**ou**d

_____   _____

- - - - - - - - - - - - -   - - - - - - - - - - - - -

_____   _____

3. j**oi**nt

_____   _____

- - - - - - - - - - - - -   - - - - - - - - - - - - -

_____   _____

4. m**oo**n

_____   _____

- - - - - - - - - - - - -   - - - - - - - - - - - - -

_____   _____

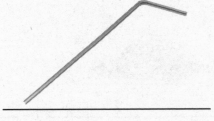

5. str**aw**

_____   _____

- - - - - - - - - - - - -   - - - - - - - - - - - - -

_____   _____

Print the words on the lines where they fit best.

1. **cou**ch

_____   _____

2. **faw**n

_____   _____

3. p**oo**l

_____   _____

4. **too**th

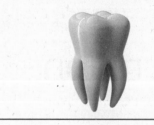

_____   _____

5. s**oi**l

_____   _____

Print the names of the things on the lines.

| hook hat | hawk hound |

_____

_____

| lap loop | coins canes |

_____

_____

| book broom | claw cloud |

_____

_____

Print the names of the things on the lines.

oil **t**o**i**l	**p**aw pan

_____

_____

sh**ou**t shack	mane m**oo**n

_____

_____

r**oo**ts r**ou**nd	t**oo**l t**oo**th

_____

_____

1. big r**oo**m   big r**oo**t

2. toss a can   toss a c**oi**n

3. lost and f**ou**nd   lost the fan

4. dr**aw** a man   dr**aw** a kid

5. red b**oo**ts   red b**oo**ks

6. l**ou**d m**ou**th   l**ou**d moth

7. a big y**aw**n   a big **law**n

8. b**oi**l fish in a pot   b**oi**l crabs in a pot

9. up and down   down and **ou**t

10. j**oi**n us at two   meet us at two

1. a big _____

2. the _____ m**oo**n

3. l**oo**k at the _____

4. bills and _____

5. t<u>wo</u> _____ c**oo**ks

6. _____ the f**oo**d

7. lunch at _____

8. a cat's _____

Dear Family Member,

This is a story your child has probably read once, possibly several times, at school. Encourage your child to read the story to you and then talk about it together. Note that the tricky parts in Tricky Words are underlined in gray.

Repeated reading is an important way to improve reading. It can be fun for your child to repeatedly read this story to a friend, relative, or even a pet.

The Fox and the Grapes

A fox **saw** a bunch of ripe grapes that hung from the branch of a tree.

The fox said, "Those grapes **loo**k g**oo**d. I will get them and make them my lunch."

The fox st**oo**d up on his back legs, but he could not grab the grapes.

The fox made a hop, but he could not grab the grapes.

The fox ran and made a big jump, but he still could not get the grapes.

At last, the fox sat down on the ground.

"What a fool I am!" said the fox. "I can tell that those grapes are sour. They would not have made a good lunch."

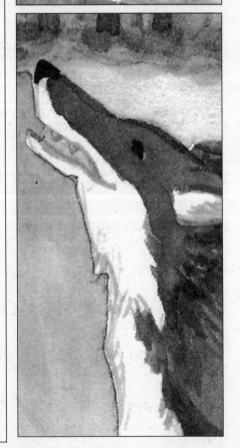

Dear Family Member,

This is a story your child has probably read once, possibly several times, at school. Encourage your child to read the story to you and then talk about it together. Note that the tricky parts in Tricky Words are underlined in gray.

Repeated reading is an important way to improve reading. It can be fun for your child to repeatedly read this story to a friend, relative, or even a pet.

The Fox and the Hen

A hen sat in a tree. A red fox ran up to the tree.

"Did they tell you?" said the fox.

"Tell me what?" said the hen.

"They have made a **law**," said the fox. The **law** says that we must all be pals. Dogs are not to chase cats. They must be pals. Cats are not to chase rats. They must be pals. Dog and cat, fox and hen, snake and rat must all be pals! So jump down here and let me hug you!"

"Well, that **sou**nds swell!" said the hen. "But, all the same, I will sit up h<u>ere</u> a bit."

Then the hen said, "What's that I see?"

"<u>Where</u>?" said the fox. "What is it?"

"It **loo**ks like a pack of dogs," said the hen.

"Dogs!" said the fox. "Then I must get **ou**t of h<u>ere</u>!"

"Stop!" said the hen. "The **law** says that dog and fox must be pals. S<u>o</u> you are safe!"

But the fox did not stop. He ran off.

The hen just smiled.

Dear Family Member,

This is a story your child has probably read once, possibly several times, at school. Encourage your child to read the story to you and then talk about it together. Note that the tricky parts in Tricky Words are underlined in gray.

Repeated reading is an important way to improve reading. It can be fun for your child to repeatedly read this story to a friend, relative, or even a pet.

The Fox and the Crane

The fox **saw** the crane and said, "Crane, will you have lunch with me?"

The crane said, "I will."

The crane came and sat down with the fox in his den.

The fox was up to a trick. He gave the crane some food, but he gave it to him in a flat stone dish. The crane could not get the

f**oo**d beca**u**s**e** of the shape of his bill. The fox smiled at his trick. He ate up all of his f**oo**d.

The next week the crane s**aw** the fox and said, "Fox, will you have lunch with m**e**?"

The fox said, "That w**ou**ld b**e** g**oo**d. I will."

This time the crane was up to a trick. He gave the fox milk, but he gave it to him in a glass with a long, thin neck. The fox c**ou**ld not get the milk beca**u**se of the shape of his nose.

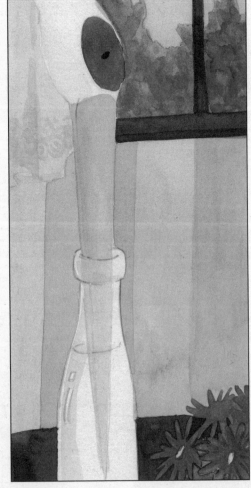

The Tree and the Reeds

Directions: Have students reread the story and answer the questions.

1. What st**oo**d next to a grove of reeds?

    _____

    _____

    _____

    _____

    Page_____

2. What did the reeds d<u>o</u> in the strong wind?

    _____

    _____

    _____

    _____

    Page_____

3. What did the tree do in the strong wind?

_____

- -

_____

_____

- -

_____

Page_____

4. Name the **noun** in: "The reeds bent."

   ○ The

   ○ reeds

   ○ bent

5. Name the **noun** in: "The tree fell."

   ○ The

   ○ tree

   ○ fell

The Moon

1. Did the m**oo**n's mom make a dress?

_____

_____

_____

_____

Page_____

2. Why can she not make a dress?

_____

_____

_____

_____

_____

Page_____

Directions: Have students reread the story and answer the questions.

3. If you c<u>ou</u>ld make a dress, what w<u>ou</u>ld it **loo**k like?

_____

_____

_____

_____

_____

_____

_____

Directions: In the box, have students draw the dress they would make.

Core Knowledge Language Arts

Series Editor-in-Chief
E. D. Hirsch, Jr.

President
Linda Bevilacqua

Editorial Staff

Carolyn Gosse, Senior Editor - Preschool
Khara Turnbull, Materials Development Manager
Michelle L. Warner, Senior Editor - Listening & Learning

Mick Anderson
Robin Blackshire
Maggie Buchanan
Paula Coyner
Sue Fulton
Sara Hunt
Erin Kist
Robin Luecke
Rosie McCormick
Cynthia Peng
Liz Pettit
Ellen Sadler
Deborah Samley
Diane Auger Smith
Sarah Zelinke

Design and Graphics Staff

Scott Ritchie, Creative Director

Kim Berrall
Michael Donegan
Liza Greene
Matt Leech
Bridget Moriarty
Lauren Pack

Consulting Project Management Services
ScribeConcepts.com

Additional Consulting Services
Ang Blanchette
Dorrit Green
Carolyn Pinkerton

Acknowledgments

These materials are the result of the work, advice, and encouragement of numerous individuals over many years. Some of those singled out here already know the depth of our gratitude; others may be surprised to find themselves thanked publicly for help they gave quietly and generously for the sake of the enterprise alone. To helpers named and unnamed we are deeply grateful.

Contributors to Earlier Versions of these Materials

Susan B. Albaugh, Kazuko Ashizawa, Nancy Braier, Kathryn M. Cummings, Michelle De Groot, Diana Espinal, Mary E. Forbes, Michael L. Ford, Ted Hirsch, Danielle Knecht, James K. Lee, Diane Henry Leipzig, Martha G. Mack, Liana Mahoney, Isabel McLean, Steve Morrison, Juliane K. Munson, Elizabeth B. Rasmussen, Laura Tortorelli, Rachael L. Shaw, Sivan B. Sherman, Miriam E. Vidaver, Catherine S. Whittington, Jeannette A. Williams

We would like to extend special recognition to Program Directors Matthew Davis and Souzanne Wright who were instrumental to the early development of this program.

Schools

We are truly grateful to the teachers, students, and administrators of the following schools for their willingness to field test these materials and for their invaluable advice: Capitol View Elementary, Challenge Foundation Academy (IN), Community Academy Public Charter School, Lake Lure Classical Academy, Lepanto Elementary School, New Holland Core Knowledge Academy, Paramount School of Excellence, Pioneer Challenge Foundation Academy, New York City PS 26R (The Carteret School), PS 30X (Wilton School), PS 50X (Clara Barton School), PS 96Q, PS 102X (Joseph O. Loretan), PS 104Q (The Bays Water), PS 214K (Michael Friedsam), PS 223Q (Lyndon B. Johnson School), PS 308K (Clara Cardwell), PS 333Q (Goldie Maple Academy), Sequoyah Elementary School, South Shore Charter Public School, Spartanburg Charter School, Steed Elementary School, Thomas Jefferson Classical Academy, Three Oaks Elementary, West Manor Elementary.

And a special thanks to the CKLA Pilot Coordinators Anita Henderson, Yasmin Lugo-Hernandez, and Susan Smith, whose suggestions and day-to-day support to teachers using these materials in their classrooms was critical.